GHOST IN THE GARDEN

D1025722

By Gail Herman

Illustrated by Duendes del Sur

SCHOLASTIC INC.

New York   Toronto   London   Auckland   Sydney
Mexico City   New Delhi   Hong Kong

No part of this work may be reproduced, stored in a retrieval system, or transmitted in any form or by any means, electronic, mechanical, photocopying, recording, or otherwise, without written permission of the publisher. For information regarding permission, write to Scholastic Inc., Attention: Permissions Department, 555 Broadway, New York, NY 10012.

ISBN 0-439-20226-4

35 34 33 32 31 30 29   40   15 16 17 18/0

Designed by Mary Hall
Printed in the U.S.A.
First Scholastic printing, October 2000

The gang was out for a drive in the Mystery Machine.

"What a great day for a ride," Fred said.

"Especially when you have a box of Scooby Snacks," Shaggy added.

"Rats right, Raggy!" said Scooby-Doo, picking up the Snacks.

Suddenly, the van went over a big bump.

"Oof!" said Shaggy.

"Roof!" said Scooby.

The Scooby Snacks flew right out the window.

"Ruh-roh!" Scooby cried.

"Stop the van!" shouted Shaggy.

Screech! Fred stopped. He backed up.

CRUNCH! He ran over the Snacks!

"What are we going to do?" Shaggy moaned.

"Like, we're starving!"

"Look up ahead!" Velma pointed to a vegetable stand in front of a farm.

"Reggies?" Scooby shook his head. "Ruh-uh."

"Well, it's not hot dogs and french fries," Shaggy agreed. "But it is better than nothing."

"Vegetables are good for you," Daphne said. "And they can be as crunchy as a Scooby Snack. How about some carrots?"
"Rummy!" said Scooby.

"Sorry," said Farmer Fran. "I am all out of carrots. I have been for days now." As she spoke she looked over her shoulder. She seemed to be afraid.

"Do you have anything else?" asked
Shaggy. As he ran over to check the baskets,
Scooby stepped on his foot.
"Ouch!" shouted Shaggy.
Farmer Fran jumped in the air. She was
afraid.

"What's wrong?" Daphne asked the farmer.
Farmer Fran sighed. "Something is taking all
the carrots and lettuce.

Every night I hear strange sounds. And when I go to check, all I see is a flash of white. I am sure there is a ghost on the farm!"

"The ghost even chased away my farm animals! I am going to leave the farm and live in the city," Farmer Fran told the gang. "I do not want to go. But what can I do? I am afraid of ghosts!"

Velma walked over to the empty cages. "Hmmm," she said. "Mystery, Inc. will investigate the mystery! Right, Scooby?" "Ro ray!" he said, looking at the empty food baskets.

"Scoob's right on," Shaggy agreed. "We're not staying at a haunted farm. Especially when there isn't any food!"

"Oh, but there is," said Farmer Fran. "How about fresh blueberry pancakes for breakfast?"

"Rokay!" said Scooby.

But that night, Scooby and Shaggy almost
changed their minds. The carrot patch was
dark and scary. And there was nowhere to
hide.

"Don't worry," said Velma. "I have an idea.
You can dress as scarecrows!"

Farmer Fran brought big dark clothes and
straw hats.
Shaggy and Scooby stuffed straw inside their
jackets and pants.

"We'll be over there." Fred pointed to a big tree. "See you later!"

Shaggy and Scooby climbed onto the fence posts.

At first, all was quiet.

"This is nice, good buddy," Shaggy said to Scooby. "Nothing like a peaceful night in the country."

Squawk! A bird landed on Scooby's shoulder.

"Rahhh!" shouted Scooby, frightened.

Shaggy laughed. "You are a scarecrow. The *bird* should be scared. Not you."

Just then a bird landed on Shaggy. "Ahh!" he shouted. Then another bird landed, then another and another.

Shaggy and Scooby shook their arms and legs. They shook their heads. The birds did not move.

All at once, they heard a rustling
sound. It was getting louder — and closer!

"Don't worry, Scoob," said Shaggy. "Nothing can get to us with these birds here."
Squawk! The birds took off.

Then Shaggy saw a flash of white — just like Farmer Fran had said.

"Okay!" Shaggy said. "This mystery is solved. There really is a ghost. Now, time for pancakes!"

He jumped off the post.
Scooby tried to jump off, too. But he was
stuck!

"Relp!" cried Scooby. He saw the flash of white again. "The rhost!" yelled Scooby. It moved closer and closer to him.

Shaggy shook Scooby's post. He pulled on his paw. He yanked on his tail. But Scooby would not come down!

"That does it!" said Shaggy. He pushed
Scooby hard. Scooby's hat flew off his head.
It landed right on the ghost!

Then Scooby flew off. *Crash!* He fell to the ground, trapping the hat between his paws.

"Scooby has the ghost!" Shaggy shouted to
the others.

"That is no ghost," said Velma. She picked up
Scooby's hat. Under the hat was a small,
white rabbit.

"What's going on?" asked Farmer Fran. Then she saw the rabbit.

"Fluffy!"

"Your ghost is just a scared little bunny," said Velma.

"The lock on her cage was broken. So she just walked out," said Fred.

"And then she ate all the carrots and lettuce," added Daphne. "Fluffy was just hungry."

Farmer Fran laughed. She picked up her bunny. "How about a midnight snack?" she asked the gang.

Scooby licked his lips.

"Great!" said Shaggy. "Blueberry pancakes with whipped cream — here we come!"

"Scooby Dooby Doo!"